Trevor Anderson and his nephew, Sean, have traveled to Iceland in search of Sean's father, Max, who believed that Jules Verne's "fictional" book, *Journey to the Center of the Earth*, was all true! There they meet Hannah, who guides them into the mountains. But a storm sends them into a cave, and a lightning bolt hits the front of the cave— *CRASH!* Rocks fall and block the entrance. The three have to search for another way out . . .

How to Use Your 3-D Glasses

Some of the images and activities in this book look fuzzy. These are 3-D images that you need special glasses to see! First tear the glasses out of the book at the perforated line. Then hold them up to your face so that your left eye is looking through the red lens and your right eye is looking through the blue lens. Now you're ready for a 3-D journey!

Runaway Mining Carts!

Trevor, Sean, and Hannah find old mining carts and tracks inside the mountain. The tracks could lead to a way out! So the three climb in and head down the trail. But wait! The track splits into three separate paths!

TRACK THE TRACKS

Trevor, Sean, and Hannah are in three carts on different paths, and they don't know where the tracks end! One set of tracks leads to a cave of sparkling gemstones—but which one? Put on your 3-D glasses to follow the tracks and find out whose cart ends up in the cave!

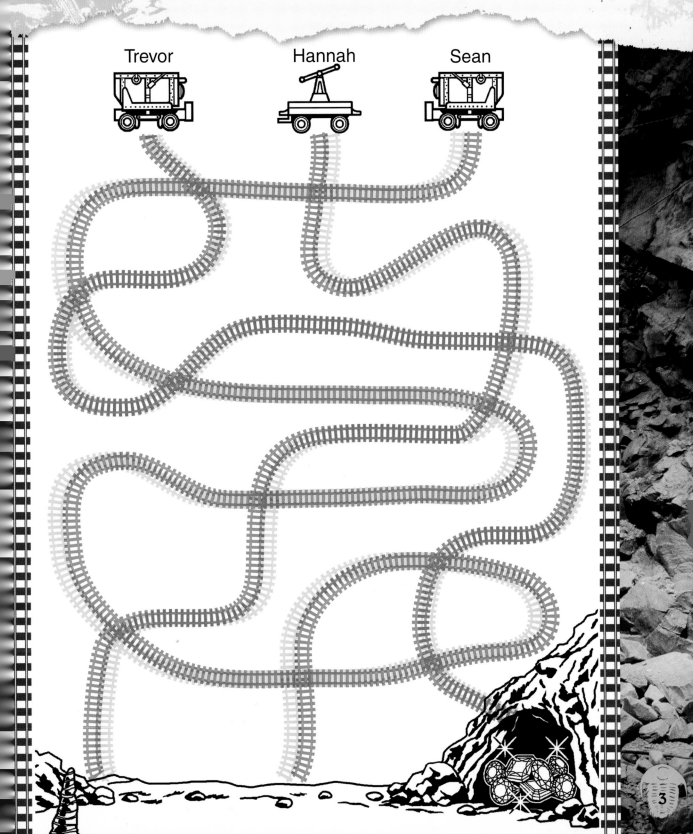

Trevor

Hannah

Sean

UNDERGROUND DISCOVERIES

They've finally made it to the center of the Earth! Hannah, Sean, and Trevor begin to explore the underground world. They discover animals that are extinct on the surface and a forest of giant mushrooms.

Earth's Hidden Secrets

The center of the Earth is full of new things for the explorers to find! Find the words in the list in the puzzle below. The words might be across, down, backward, forward, or diagonal!

Word List:

DIAMONDS

ARCHAEOPTERYX

MUSHROOMS

JOURNAL

TRILOBITE

COMPASS

PTERICHTHYS

GIGANTOSAURUS

MAGNETS

LAVA

```
S  K  D  G  X  A  T  J  M  Z  A  N  E  R  R
J  U  A  J  O  U  R  N  A  L  E  G  N  P  S
L  A  R  R  X  R  E  T  P  X  U  R  I  B  V
V  A  M  U  C  M  U  S  H  R  O  O  M  S  C
T  X  V  O  A  H  D  I  A  M  O  N  D  S  R
A  R  Z  A  R  S  A  W  P  R  P  H  N  P  N
F  V  I  J  W  X  O  E  G  P  H  A  V  Y  J
I  E  I  L  J  U  H  T  O  W  D  T  M  H  B
M  I  M  B  O  I  W  O  N  P  Q  H  G  Y  V
A  Y  N  O  W  B  Z  L  W  A  T  I  N  B  I
G  M  P  O  P  J  I  N  O  L  G  E  K  X  S
N  F  L  K  T  H  V  T  W  A  E  I  R  C  B
E  R  J  A  J  A  F  Y  E  H  I  I  G  Y  V
T  P  T  E  R  I  C  H  T  H  Y  S  T  L  X
S  M  X  J  S  S  A  P  M  O  C  R  P  S  H
```

Treacherous Travels

Sean has gotten lost, and he needs to find his way back to Uncle Trevor! But to get there, he has to cross a huge canyon. Fortunately there are stepping stones for him to walk across—but the rocks are suspended in midair by magnetism!

MAGNETIC MAZE

Help Sean find his way across the canyon on the magnetic rocks!
Put on your 3-D glasses and find the shortest path across the stones.

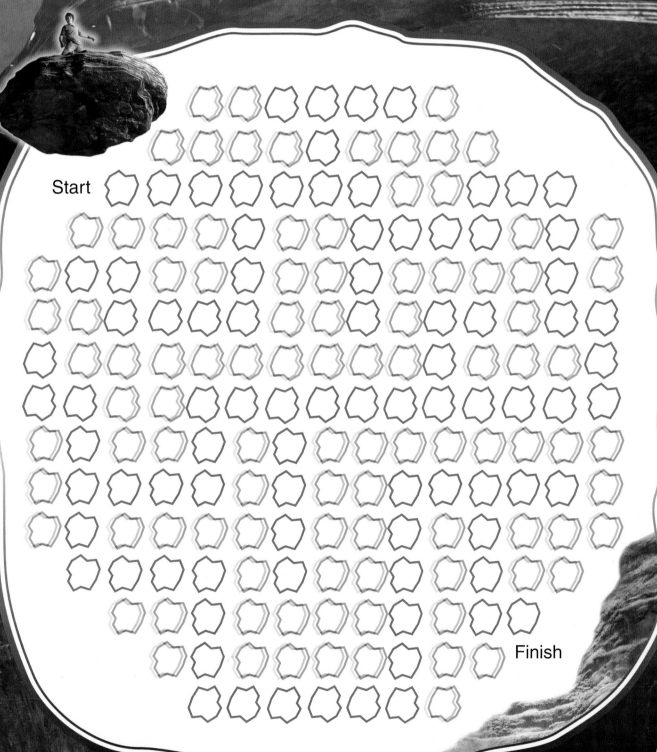

Start

Finish

7

Run for

GIGANTOSAURUS!

A hungry albino gigantosaurus is after Sean and Trevor! The huge dinosaur chases them through the underground world—and they have nowhere to hide! But Trevor sees ground made of muscovite ahead. If he can trick the dinosaur to run onto the fragile ground, they might be able to escape!

DINOSAUR DANGER

Trevor needs to get the gigantosaurus onto the muscovite without falling through himself! Put on your 3-D glasses and follow the maze to find a safe route for Trevor to follow. But be careful to avoid the dinosaur!

Start

Finish

Row, Row, Row Your Boat?

Sean, Trevor, and Hannah need to follow the underground river to a geyser. The water in the geyser should be strong enough to shoot the three explorers back to the surface! Hannah finds a gigantic dinosaur skull to use as a boat.

JOURNEY WORDS

How much do you know about *Journey to the Center of the Earth 3D*? Find out by filling in the crossword puzzle below! The answers can all be found inside this book!

DOWN

1. Country where Trevor, Sean, and Hannah entered the center of the Earth.

2. Author of *Journey to the Center of the Earth*: Jules _____.

3. The force that caused giant rocks in the center of the Earth to float in midair.

4. Sean's Dad's name: _____ Anderson.

ACROSS

1. Country where Trevor, Sean, and Hannah come out above ground.

3. The three travelers found a forest of _____.

5. What 3-D stands for: three-_____.

6. The fragile mineral that the gigantosaurus fell through.

BACK TO THE SURFACE

Trevor, Sean, and Hannah are almost out, but they need your help! Put on your 3-D glasses and find a path for the explorers from the center of the Earth out to the surface.

Start

Finish

They finally made it back! Hannah, Trevor, and Sean crash through a vineyard in their dinosaur-skull boat after they're blown out of the mountain. Trevor turns around to see that they've come out of Mount Vesuvius—they're in Italy!

Home, Sweet Home

Trevor, Sean, and Hannah are safely back on the surface. Sean heads home to his mom in Canada, and Hannah returns to the United States with Trevor. And thanks to Sean grabbing some diamonds underground, Trevor and Hannah have enough money to open their own scientific laboratory and continue researching the world at the center of the Earth!

Awesome A

Letters come in big and small sizes! The big form of each letter is called uppercase. The small form of each letter is called lowercase.

A and **a** are letter partners.

  Trace each **A** and **a**. Then write some of your own.

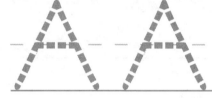

 Color each picture whose name begins with **a**.

apple

Bert

ant

1

Bouncing with B

B and **b** are letter partners.

  Trace each **B** and **b**. Then write some of your own.

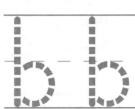

 Circle each picture whose name begins with **b**.

fan   **bat**   **ball**

C Is for Cookie

C and **c** are letter partners.

 Trace each **C** and **c**. Then write some of your own.

 Color each picture whose name begins with **c**.

sun   **carrot**   **cake**

(3)

Dandy Letter D

D and **d** are letter partners.

  Trace each **D** and **d**. Then write some of your own.

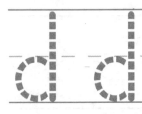

 Circle each picture whose name begins with **d**.

door

tree

drum

4

Excellent E

E and **e** are letter partners.

  Trace each **E** and **e**. Then write some of your own.

 Color each picture whose name begins with **e**.

  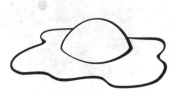

envelope   **dog**   **egg**

F and **f** are letter partners.

  Trace each **F** and **f**. Then write some of your own.

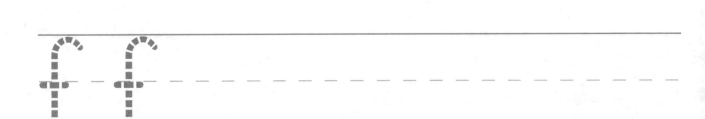

 Circle each picture whose name begins with **f**.

fish **book** **five**

G Is Great

G and **g** are letter partners.

  Trace each **G** and **g**. Then write some of your own.

 Color each picture whose name begins with **g**.

gate   **bottle**   **grapes**

Hats off for H

 **H** **h**

H and **h** are letter partners.

  Trace each **H** and **h**. Then write some of your own.

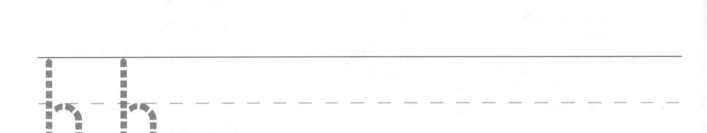

H H

h h

 Circle each picture whose name begins with **h.**

kitten **hammer** **hat**

 8

Incredible I

I and i are letter partners.

 Trace each **I** and **i**. Then write some of your own.

 Color each picture whose name begins with **i**.

igloo　　　　**cow**　　　　**ink**

Gg-Hh-Ii Hunt

Help Elmo find the hidden letters.

Find and circle **G**, **H**, and **I**.
Then find and circle **g**, **h**, and **i**.

Jumping for J

J and **j** are letter partners.

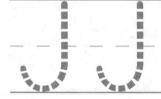 Trace each **J** and **j**. Then write some of your own.

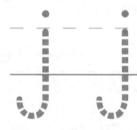

 Circle each picture whose name begins with **j**.

duck

jacket

jar

11

Alphabet with Elmo   **SESAME STREET**

| **K** | **k** |

K and **k** are letter partners.

 Trace each **K** and **k**.
Then write some of your own.

 Color each picture whose name begins with **k**.

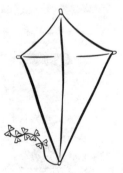

kite   **key**   **bee**

Look out for L

L and **l** are letter partners.

 Trace each **L** and **l**. Then write some of your own.

L L

 Circle each picture whose name begins with **l**.

lamp

lion

frog

Alphabet with Elmo **SESAME STREET**

M **m**

M and **m** are letter partners.

 Trace each **M** and **m**. Then write some of your own.

 Color each picture whose name begins with **m**.

moon   **mitten**   **leaf**

14

N Is Very Nice

N and **n** are letter partners.

 Trace each **N** and **n**.
Then write some of your own.

NN

nn

Circle each picture whose name begins with **n**.

nail

mouse

nine

15

O Is Out of This World

O and **o** are letter partners.

 Trace each **O** and **o**. Then write some of your own.

 Color each picture whose name begins with **o**.

octopus **Grover** **owl**

 16

SESAME STREET Alphabet with Elmo

Perfectly P

P and **p** are letter partners.

 Trace each **P** and **p**. Then write some of your own.

 Circle each picture whose name begins with **p**.

tire

pear

pie

Alphabet with Elmo

Q and **q** are letter partners.

  Trace each **Q** and **q**. Then write some of your own.

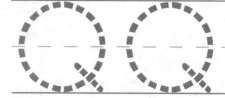

 Color each picture whose name begins with **q**.

queen   **Rosita**   **quilt**

 18

Remarkable R

  R **r**

R and **r** are letter partners.

 Trace each **R** and **r**. Then write some of your own.

 R R

r r

 Circle each picture whose name begins with **r**.

cup   **robe**   **rug**

S and **s** are letter partners.

  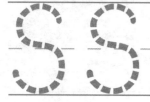

Trace each **S** and **s**.
Then write some of your own.

_____

_____

 Color each picture whose name begins with **s**.

snake　　　　　**seal**　　　　　**car**

Terrific T

T and **t** are letter partners.

  Trace each **T** and **t**. Then write some of your own.

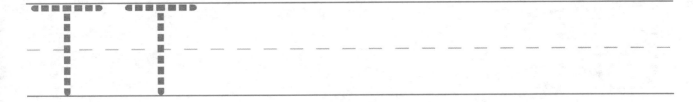

 Circle each picture whose name begins with **t**.

truck   **plane**   **turtle**

Unique U

U and **u** are letter partners.

 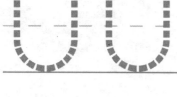 Trace each **U** and **u**.
Then write some of your own.

 Color each picture whose name begins with **u**.

unicorn

pillow

umbrella

Valuable V

V and **v** are letter partners.

  Trace each **V** and **v**.
Then write some of your own.

V V

v v

 Circle each picture whose name begins with **v**.

Snuffy   **van**   **vase**

Alphabet with Elmo   SESAME STREET

Wonderful W

W and **w** are letter partners.

  Trace each **W** and **w**.
Then write some of your own.

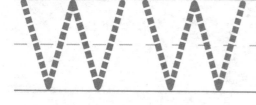

WW

ww

 Color each picture whose name begins with **w**.

watch   **well**   **mop**

(24)

X–tra Special X

X and **x** are letter partners.

 Trace each **X** and **x**. Then write some of your own.

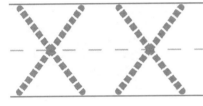

 Circle each picture whose name begins with **x**.

xylophone

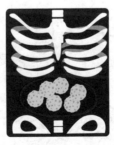

x-ray

fish

Alphabet with Elmo SESAME STREET

Yippee for Y

Y and **y** are letter partners.

 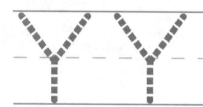 Trace each **Y** and **y**.
Then write some of your own.

Y Y

y y

 Color each picture whose name begins with **y**.

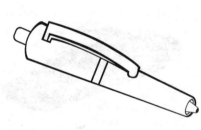

yogurt　　　　　**yak**　　　　　**pen**

Zany About Z

Z and z are letter partners.

  Trace each **Z** and **z**.
Then write some of your own.

Z Z

z z

 Circle each picture whose name begins with **z**.

zebra　　　　**Elmo**　　　　**zero**

27

Practice A to Z

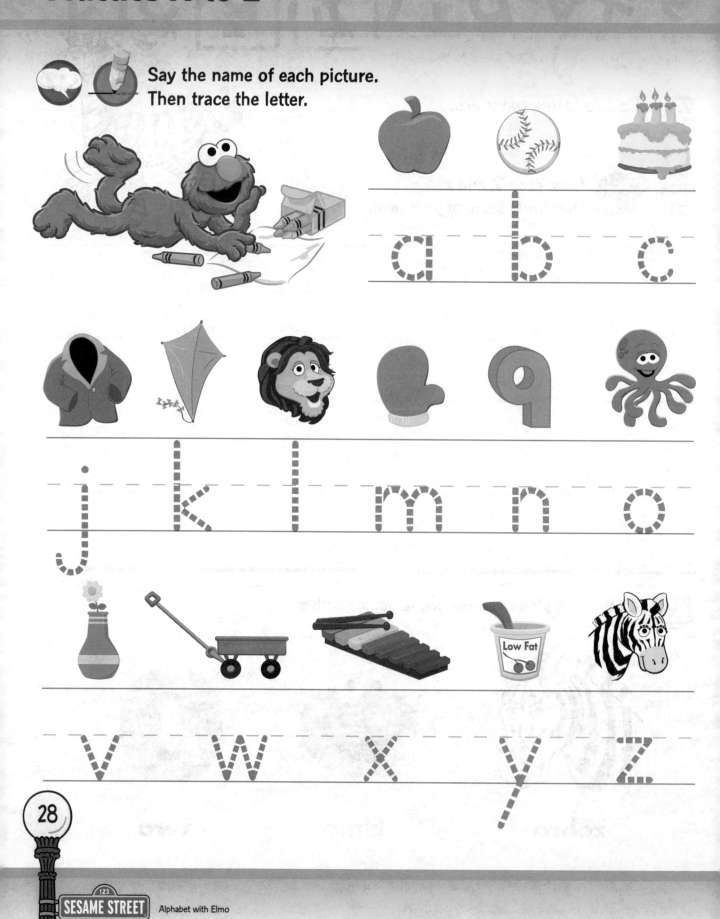

Say the name of each picture.
Then trace the letter.

a   b   c

j   k   l   m   n   o

v   w   x   y   z

d e f g h i

p q r s t u

29

Super Letter Maze

Help Cookie Monster and Prairie Dawn go from **Aa** to **Zz**.

 Draw a line through the path that shows letter partners.

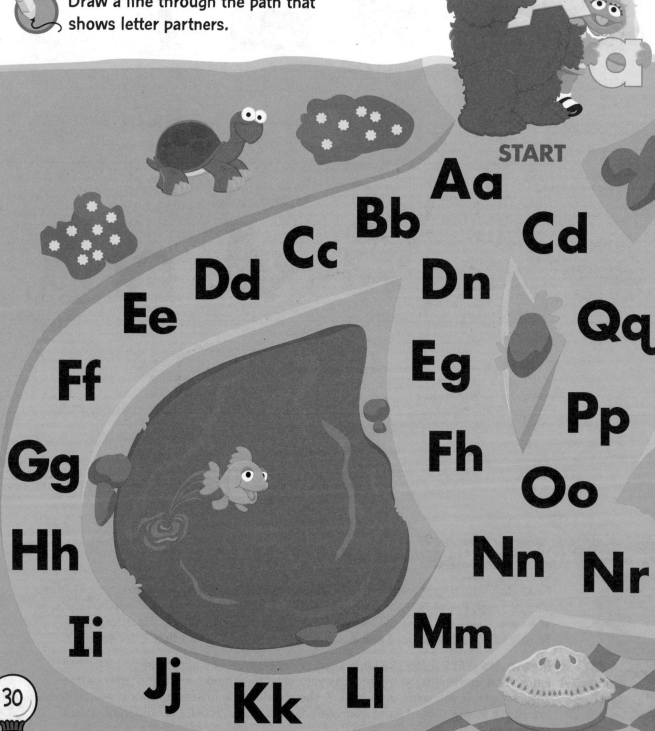

START

Aa

Bb

Cc

Cd

Dd

Dn

Ee

Eg

Qq

Ff

Fh

Pp

Gg

Oo

Hh

Nn

Nr

Ii

Mm

Jj

Kk

Ll

30

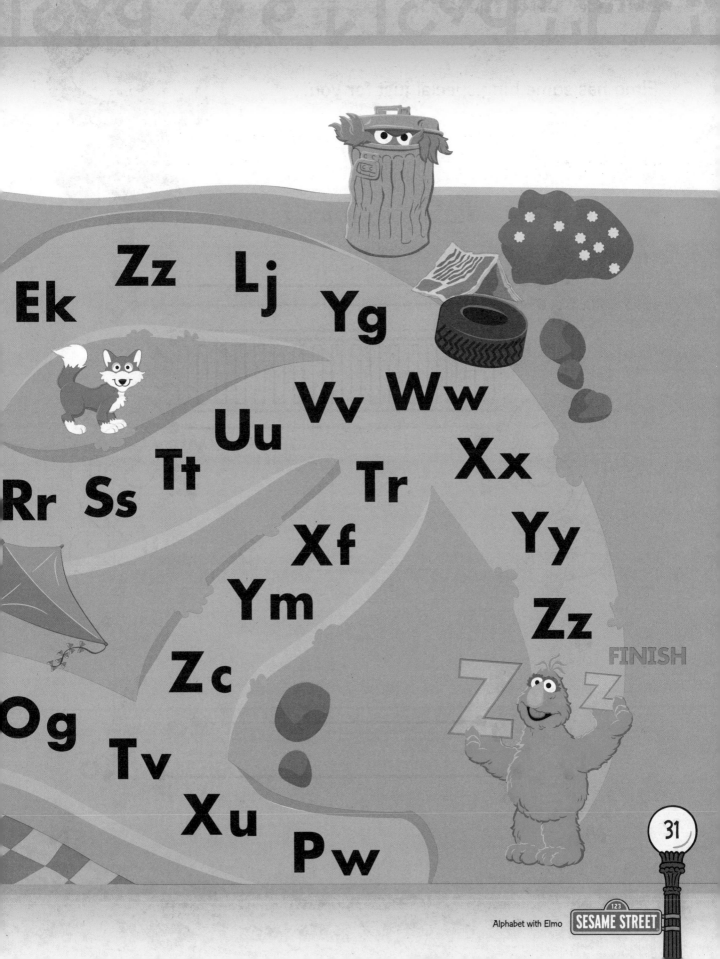

Ek Zz Lj Yg

Vv Ww

Uu

Tt Tr Xx

Rr Ss Xf Yy

Ym Zz

Zc FINISH

Og

Tv

Xu Pw

31

Alphabet with Elmo   SESAME STREET

Letter Champion

Elmo has something special just for you!

 Draw lines to connect the dots from **A** to **Z**.

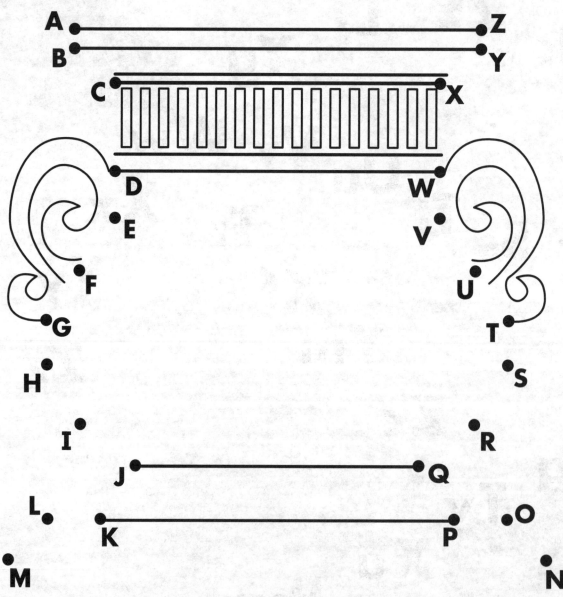

A • ———————————————— • Z
B • ———————————————— • Y
C •   • X
D •   • W
  • E   V •
    • F   U •
  • G   • T
H •   • S
  • I   • R
    J • ———————————— • Q
L •   • O
  • K ———————————— • P
• M   • N